Carol Weis

Ard Hoyt

WHEN THE COWS GOT
LOOSE

Simon & Schuster Books for Young Readers

New York   London   Toronto   Sydney

THE DAY THE COWS GOT LOOSE, Granny was taking her weekly soak in the tub, and Grampy was knitting the last row on his purple scarf.

The day the cows got loose, Ma was out back choppin' a load of wood, and Pa was mending a hole in the roof of the chicken coop. Good ol' Calliope was buryin' a bone by the back door.

The day the cows got loose, I was hanging upside down in the ol' apple tree, dreamin' about how to git famous someday. Pa said since I watched them cows cut loose, I could round 'em up. All twenty-six of 'em.

I let out a big sigh, so's Pa could hear, and moseyed over to Mrs. Henshaw's.

I knew Alberta and Betty would be there.
They love Mrs. Henshaw's cabbages.

On our way back home, we passed Mr. Andrew's place. The chairs
were missin' from his front porch.
Seems Zora had something to do with it.

Who'd a thought?

Next morning, while I was fryin' up a couple of ol' Gilly's eggs, Pa got a call from Mrs. McGrath. I could hear her shouting from clear across the room. He held out the phone, looked at me and said, "Ida Mae, Mrs. McGrath wants to take her morning swim."

I cooked up those eggs . . .

then skipped down to McGrath's, with Calli at my heels.

Sure enough, there was Candy and Dotty doin' ballet
smack-dab in the middle of Mrs. McGrath's pool.
"Looky here, Cal. Come on, we're goin' swimmin'."
I held my nose and jumped in.

Toward evenin', got a call from Aunt Mary. Cousin William was at the swamp today and so were Yolanda, Ellie, Fannie, Xenia, and Greta.

"Sakes alive, Calli, I got to see this."
So I hopped on my bike and headed for the swamp.

"Well, I'll be . . ."

That night I fell asleep and dreamed about Hildegarde and
Winifred, eatin' their way through the Howards' haystack. They
had blown up like balloons and were floating over their cornfield.

Next day I got up before the rooster, Roustabout, and whistled for Calli.

"But Hilde doesn't like corn. She likes clover," I said, as we tumbled over to the Howards'.

No sign of Hildegarde and Winifred.

By the time we got to the Neilsons' farm, where the sweetest clover grows, the sun was rubbin' its sleepy eyes and, I'll be, those little heifers were already gone.

So we wandered over to the Siversens' and there they were,
hopping in the haystacks.

"This is gooder 'n grits."

Weren't eatin' like I reckoned. After takin' a few jumps myself, I
hauled those zany creatures home.

That afternoon, while shootin' a game of marbles with Grampy on the front porch, we got another call. This time from Mr. Dewey. Says there was a car settin' in front of his house. Seems that Irene, Jeanette, Violet, Katie, Lucy, and Ursula were up to something. Before Pa even hung up that phone, he was sayin', "Ida Mae, best get to the Deweys'."

Calli and I dallied on down to the Deweys'.

"Well, knock me down."

Spent the best part of the afternoon tryin' to get those cows out of that car. When they finally tuckered out, I herded them home.

The followin' night, right about the time I was settling into a good game of checkers with Granny, you guessed it, the phone rang.

"Howdy, Mr. Simpson. Gee, I'm sorry, Mr. Simpson. She'll be right down, Mr. Simpson." Granny let out a big sigh. She had just kinged her first checker.

I grabbed the lantern and stomped out the door.

Seems Mr. Simpson had a troop of those critters roamin' round his backyard. Saw them when he called his kitty in for the night. Scared the daylights out of him.

Mad as I was at havin' my checker game disturbed, I couldn't help
starin' when I saw Minerva, Nelly, and Tilly tiptoein' across
Mr. Simpson's clothesline decked out in Mr. Simpson's clean sheets.

Knew Tilly would follow the lantern. First thing she saw the night she was birthed.

After that, no calls for three days. Pa started pacin' and twistin' his cap.

"Ida Mae, enough of this clowning around," he said. "Turn off that Victrola and go find that last batch of bovine."

"Aw, Pa," I said. I didn't want to int'rupt my dancin', but I could tell he meant business.

So Calli and I headed straight for the apple tree, where we do our best thinkin'. "Well, Calli, there's twenty-six cows that live in that there barn and I rounded up twenty-one. Who's left? There's Ophelia, Pauline, and Susie Q. They like the breeze beatin' down on their brows. Queenie and Renee. What in tarnation do they like, Calli?"

Calli jumped up on the swing.

"Shoot, dang," I said, "they like high places. Why didn't I think of that? Let's go get Pa."

We hopped in Pa's truck and
motored over to Mizz Romano's.

When Pa caught sight of Ophelia, Pauline, Susie Q, Queenie, Renee, and Mizz Romano, he took off his cap, scratched his head, and said, "Now, don't that just beat all."

The day we finished roundin' up the cows, on the first a Ju-ly, Granny was taking her weekly soak in the tub, and Grampy was modeling his new purple scarf. Ma was out back stacking a load a wood, while Pa was in the chicken coop, gathering eggs.

As for me, I was hanging upside down in the ol' apple tree, dreamin' about how to git famous someday. . . .

TO MY DEAR MAGGIE, WHO STOOD AT THE WINDOW AND WATCHED WITH ME,
THE DAY THE COWS GOT LOOSE—C. W.

TO MY JEWEL, SAGE, BEAUTIFUL AND BRAVE—A. H.

Acknowledgments

An armful of hugs to the following people for their love and support: my daughter, Maggie Henley; the members of my writing group, Linda Shaughnessy, Nance Carpenter, Elaine Streeter, and Tom McCabe; my sister, Sui, and her husband, Phil; my mom, Betty; my brothers, John and Phil; Jimmy; my friends, Laurie, Burleigh, Sue R., Joanie, Leslie, Trina, Sue T., and Lennie; Maggie's Dad, Martin, and her grandpa, Dewey; Aunt El and Uncle Chet; my team of healers, Renee, Marcia and Lisa; the staff at Edward's Library; Jane Yolen and the Hatfield writing group; and most certainly, Kevin, Alyssa, and Joanna, without whose loving attention this book would not exist. And let's not forget the cows of Wolf Hill Farm.—C. W.

SIMON & SCHUSTER BOOKS FOR YOUNG READERS
An imprint of Simon & Schuster Children's Publishing Division
1230 Avenue of the Americas, New York, New York 10020
Text copyright © 2006 by Carol Weis
Illustrations copyright © 2006 by Ard Hoyt
SIMON & SCHUSTER BOOKS FOR YOUNG READERS is a trademark of Simon & Schuster, Inc.
Book design by Daniel Roode
The text for this book is set in ACaslon Regular.
The illustrations for this book are rendered in watercolor, colored pencil, pen, and ink.
Manufactured in China
2 4 6 8 10 9 7 5 3 1
CIP data for this book is available from the Library of Congress.
ISBN-13: 978-0-689-85166-7
ISBN-10: 0-689-85166-9